The Witch Hunter

Richard Poche

Published by Richard Poche, 2021.

THE WITCH HUNTER

First edition. July 15, 2021.

Copyright © 2021 Richard Poche.

ISBN: 979-8224661244

Written by Richard Poche.

WITCH HUNTER
BOOK ONE OF WITCH MASTERS

RICHARD POCHE

CHAPTER ONE

Maddy's heartbeat rose and pounded.

She hated that about herself. Always a nervous wreck whenever faced with the slightest challenge.

She had gone to journalism school. She knew how to conduct an interview. The things to ask and not to ask.

Still, her heart beat even faster as she listened to the ringing dial, trying to block out all of the activity around her. The horrible rap music Olivia played in the cubicle over, the fingers tapping on keyboards, and all of the different kinds of beeps and buttons going off in the office. Maddy always felt a sense of overstimulation during times of stress.

She wanted to impress on her first assignment. Sounded easy enough. All she had to do was write a decent obituary article on the wife of a popular local restaurant owner. Bill Mosley had started "Bill's Grill" from scratch and had been featured on one of the shows on the Food Network. The man knew chili inside and out, even becoming semi-famous for it.

But his wife, Patricia, remained a mystery.

Until she died. Now Maddy's editor thought it only natural that the town paper did a more substantial piece on the rich man's wife. Mosley himself agreed.

Maddy had rehearsed what to say. She would tell him how sorry she felt at his loss and—

"Bill Mosley," the voice answered on the other end.

"Mr. Mosley," Maddy scrambled to focus her thoughts. "Sir, this is Maddy Stoner of the *Alameda Chronicle*. I'm calling about writing an article on—"

"Oh God," Mosley mumbled. "Yeah, that. Oh, just write what you want as long as I get sympathy. I just don't want it to look bad that there isn't anything in the paper about her death. That would be bad for business."

"We'll have quite a lot of ground to cover. You wanted a full page?"

"I guess," Mosley chuckled. "Do people even read the newspaper anymore? I want as many people to see it as possible. I want them to feel sorry for me and not be such assholes when my new chef gives them diarrhea."

"Yes," Maddy said, ignoring the joke. "Anything in particular we should focus on? I have a list of items we can go through?"

"I'm just trying to forget about her," Mosley's voice became somber. "I mean, Jesus. You can keep it simple. Sunrise 1960. Sunset 2020. I sent you folks a picture of her. Taken years ago before she became a walrus."

"I can certainly detail her life—" Maddy could hear the tinkle of a shot glass and Mosley slurping the liquor down.

"Look," Mosley belched like a sleeping hippo awakening. "The woman was nuts. The cheese slid off her cracker years ago. Got into all this woo occult shit and called herself a witch. I swear for years we'd argue and argue, and she told me she would cast a spell on me. Said she'd put a curse on my ass and I'd die taking a shit like Elvis. Well, I think the spell backfired."

Mosley laughed hard, then began coughing.

"Mister Mosley?" Maddy asked after the hacking died down.

"Sorry, sorry," he continued. "Found her spread-eagled on the can. The bathroom smelled like a thousand assholes by the time the coroner got here. Almost as bad as her perfume."

"Sorry to hear that," Maddy offered.

"I'll tell you on the square," Mosley's voice turned somber. "I should have divorced that whack job years ago. We went to a marriage counselor once. Guy gave us a piece of paper with a list of questions about the other person. Standard stuff. What was their favorite food? Favorite kind of music? TV show? Well, I was able to answer about ninety percent of the questions and hand the paper back to him. A day later, he called me back into his office and wanted me to come alone. Showed me the piece of paper that she filled out. She didn't even know anything about me.

Filled about two of twenty questions right. The rest she left blank! The marriage counselor looked at me and said, "Get rid of this bitch while you still can. She doesn't give a damn about you." But I didn't listen. I didn't listen. Maybe that was the spell she had on me."

"Sorry to hear that," Maddy said, now feeling the need to take control of the conversation. "I'm wondering if we can focus on the positive things about her though?"

"Positive?" Mosley laughed so loud that the sound hurt Maddy's ears.

"Like what were the things you answered in that questionnaire about her? Her favorite food? Music? Her hobbies? Those sorts of things can help me write an obituary that would help those who want to remember her."

"I'm just trying to forget," Mosley chuckled again. "Her only hobby was that Witch Club she belonged to. Raven Heights or whatever. They thought she was the queen bee or something. She just memorized a bunch of shit from a book. Mother-in-law was bat shit crazy too. You can write that she was a witch that finally got on her broom and flew their asses straight back to hell where they came from."

Maddy tried to get as much information as she could out of Bill Mosley, but the man continued to refuse to answer her questions directly. He railed against his deceased wife and kept repeating how much he now looked forward to urinating on her grave.

After fifteen minutes of fruitless back and forth, Maddy looked down at her scribbled notes culled from talking to neighbors and what few friends she could find. Patricia Mosley didn't come across as a particularly likable figure. An apparently abusive woman who practiced witchcraft, rarely bathed, and reeked of cheap perfume.

And a pain-in-the-ass to the man she married.

Looking up from her desk, Maddy saw her own pain-in-the-ass walking down the office aisle.

Kelly, the office bully slash coordinator.

Maddy knew what was coming. Her father had been a former boxer and always lamented that the punches that hurt the most were the ones you didn't see coming. He told her that story as sort of a parable to prepare Maddy for the curves life would throw at her. But Maddy disagreed. The punches were coming, and she could see them from a mile away in the form of Kelly. She walked with a bounce in her step, making sure the young man that pushed the mail cart around the office noticed her jiggling bosom. That and her long eyelashes that blinked across green eyes were the smoke and mirrors that hid her passive-aggressive agenda.

The office staff at the *Alameda Chronicle* had been dwindling for the past couple of years, Maddy had been told. Standing in a five-story building, a testament to the influence and reach it once had, the mail boy still went to every floor.

Maddy could only watch as the office flirt swooped down on the shy, acne-inflicted young man like a hawk on a mouse.

"You're such a hard-working man," Kelly said in a breathy whisper, emphasizing the word hard. "Lemme save your legs."

Without warning, she took the bundle of mail from his cart and began thumbing through it.

Maddy watched as Kelly's face contorted into a wide smile when she found her prize.

"Madusa Stoner," she called out, attracting the attention of everyone in the office. "Mail for Madusa Stoner."

She sauntered over to Maddy's desk and tossed the mail upon it, her eyes shining but not in good fun. Maddy had no idea what she'd done to attract the hostile attention of this young woman, but it felt as if from her very first day, Kelly's eyes had glinted with excited malice every time she'd glanced in Maddy's direction. Her name had only provided her with more fodder for her constant teasing as she called it, although to Maddy it felt more like harassment or outright bullying.

"Thanks," Maddy forced a smile.

"Don't thank me, Madusa," Kelly replied with a giggle. "Thank your parents."

"I go by Maddy."

Kelly stood loitering at Maddy's cubicle, appraising her appearance with a mocking look on her face. "You know," Kelly said, picking up a fantasy novel off Maddy's desk, "You look like one of those villagers they always show in those Salem Witch Trial documentaries. You're nondescript. Plain. I mean, I bet you could squeeze out fart after fart and not change your facial expression."

Kelly dropped the book on the floor, spun around, and entered the three-employee cubicle across from Maddy. Inside, Kent and Clifton eyed her like hopeful puppies. Maddy's hypersensitive ears could hear Kelly's insults and the young men laughing only to get into Kelly's good graces. The only woman in the cubicle, Olivia, stood up and walked away. Kent and Clifton looked back at Maddy with cold eyes, then back at Kelly with submissive fascination.

Maddy picked her book up from the floor and turned her attention to the mail that landed on her desk, trying to quell the anger pounding in her heart. She inherited her dad's sensitivity to insults but also her mother's passivity. A combination which often led her to suffer in silence.

The narrative of her life which perhaps had become something she could thank her parents for as well.

She'd been so excited about starting the job. She'd wanted to be a writer all of her life. Fiction, non-fiction, or news journalism, it didn't matter. Getting a foot in the door at the *Alameda Chronicle* as soon as she'd graduated had been massive, even if it were only to type up the small jobs. She had to start somewhere and saw the job as a great starting point. One step on the rung to fulfilling her lifelong dream. Now, here at the end of her first week, she realized another maxim that her father had once said.

You can't escape stupid people.

But damn, working here already felt as if she were back in junior high.

And she still had to sell Allie on this town.

CHAPTER TWO

"Are you nervous about going to a new school?" Maddy looked over at her younger sister, Allie, with concern.

"No," Allie kept staring out the window. "Besides, I really won't be there very long."

"We can drive by just so you can see what it looks like."

"I already looked it up," Allie said. "A school is a school."

"Welcome to your new hometown," Maddy pointed at a sign that said, "Welcome to Alameda.

To her relief, her little sister was looking out the windows at the passing scenery with bright curiosity. At just seventeen years of age, Maddy wouldn't have been surprised if she'd been sitting with folded arms, earbuds in, and a sulky pout on her face. "It's nice," Allie replied, peering at the small boutiques on the right-hand side of the street. "Different from home."

"See? New place and new adventure. You're not mad at me for dragging you out here?"

Allie shook her head. "No. Besides, if I'd stayed, I'd end up just like everyone else. Working in retail or a factory and never leaving. Out here? It feels, well, it feels as if there are possibilities."

"Remember, things are only a dead end if you make them that way. Wherever we're at, we're going to be happy, right?"

Allie gave her sister a tight smile, which gave Maddy some relief. Ever since their parents had been killed in a car accident just over a year ago, the sisters had only had one another. They'd never known any other family and presumed that that was the way their parents wanted it. None had come out of the woodwork after their death, and they hadn't gone looking for them.

"As Dad would say," Allie said, "Stoners against the world."

"Yeah, he would say that."

They giggled, but Maddy's laugh quickly subsided. They had been spared growing up in the city, spared the kind of mean teasing and hazing that afflicted so many teens Allie's age. Maddy privately crossed her fingers that the people here would be as friendly as they were in their rural town, for her sister's sake. God forbid they were the same as her co-workers.

"Leaving was hard." Allie looked out the window at the long stretch of grass in front of a junior college. "Dina didn't want me to go. She hugged me for so long. Felt like, forever."

"And Tim?"

"He played it cool." Allie shook her head. "Until the end. I could see water in his eyes. Said he'd write. You know. Still keep in touch. Phone calls. Facebook. Who knows how long that will last?"

"It'll fade out," Maddy said. "You'll meet new people. Then you'll get old and get nostalgia for one another. But that's all it will ever be."

"Jesus, you're depressing."

"No," Maddy laughed, taking her hand off the wheel and play hitting Allie's shoulder. "I'm happy. Happy wherever and whenever."

The two laughed, then drove in silence for minutes, turning the corner and making their way onto a long strip with a beach on their right side.

"It looks like a painting." Allie sat up as the sight of the bay piqued her curiosity. The California summer sun glistened off the waters, making it sparkle like crystal.

"I like the colors. It's green with a bluish tinge. Mom would have liked painting it."

"God, yes."

"Right?"

"You know what the toughest part of coming here is?" Allie asked. "It's leaving Mom and Dad there. Their graves. Not like we would have ever visited."

"We would have."

"No." Allie's sparkling eyes now dissolved into a faraway stare. "It would have been too painful."

"This is what they would have wanted."

"You said that three times already."

"Maybe I didn't say it right. We would have gotten comfortable there. Too comfortable. I mean, look at Dina's mom. Not to be mean, but she's happy and content with her life. And she's as dumb as a brick."

"She was nice."

"Never ventured out of that little street," Maddy continued. "The perfect example of how ignorance is bliss. Now, by us moving here, we don't have to wonder. We can see the world. We can explore. Wait until I show you San Francisco."

Maddy watched as Allie turned away from the sight of the bay and closed her eyes. She knew that look, that Allie had been listening but not hearing her. She knew that Allie had images of rolling hills, old friends, and outings with her parents as a family flickering in her mind. Allie's peers would seem like children to her now after what she went through.

Allie's eyes opened as they passed a sushi restaurant on the main strip of the city.

"Sushi," Allie said. "Remember, we only had it that one time and talked about it ever since. Maybe I can get a waitress job there and double-dip on the food and get some big city tips. You know, help us out."

"Or save it for college," Maddy gave another smile of relief, impressed that her sister would be willing to help out and contribute to living expenses.

"Oh, I'll easily find a job to pay my way then," Allie said with a wave of her hand. "Right now, I'm thinking about décor and furnishings. I think we did the right thing putting most of the stuff from the old house into storage—fresh start and all that—but I know replacing it all is going to make money tight."

"Well, the place came partially furnished, so I had all the basics. It'll be up to us to add our own touches and make it a real home." Maddy pulled up into a short, narrow driveway and turned off the engine. "What do you think?"

She practically held her breath as she watched Allie peer out of the windshield of the car at the little house in front of them. She had ditched her one-bedroom apartment in nearby Oakland for this small two-bedroom home once Allie agreed to come move in with her.

A cute one-story with a wraparound porch, the wooden construction had been painted a sunny, cheerful yellow. Maddy had felt drawn to it when she'd seen it online on the realtor's website. It looked out of place in the city, like something you would find in their small town. By some miracle, she found a place where the rent wouldn't bite too much into the meager income she would have from the newspaper.

"Looks cozy," Allie said. "I like it!"

~*~

Maddy gave Allie a guided tour of the main street, showcasing the ethnic diversity of Himalayan, French, Moroccan, and Ethiopian cuisine, just to name a few offerings. But Allie decided on her favorite meal. Jumbo Jacks from Jack in the Box and French fries from McDonald's.

"I swear," Allie said between bites. "They should just combine Jack in the Box with McDonald's. I mean, Jack in the Box has the better burgers. But McDonald's has the best fries."

"Combine the two?" Maddy said, picking out a small tomato slice from her McSalad Shaker.

"Yeah. Like, call it Mack in the Box or JackDonalds."

They finished their early dinner and began unpacking Allie's belongings from the SUV. She had traveled light and only brought along the essentials.

Well, almost.

Maddy opened the box of old pictures and almost shuddered. The past thirteen months had been tough after their parent's tragic accident. She had had an initial outburst of grief followed by a period of pure numbness. She didn't allow herself to think of her mother or father. Forcing herself to move on, she focused on her studies and her new job.

She had been successful in controlling her grief until she'd opened the box of pictures.

"I figured we could put them on whatever mantelpiece you have," Allie smiled at Maddy before scanning her eyes around the room for a suitable spot. "But I have never seen so many books in my life. Did you move away just so you had room to put your books?"

"Yeah, maybe." Maddy looked around her home. The girl had her pegged. She had one shelf dedicated to fiction, separated by genre. A lot of Stephen King and Dean Koontz, plus another shelf dedicated to self-help. If she ever brought a date home, he would have her figured out just by checking out the books on the wall.

"How about here?" Allie asked, taking an old picture of their parents posing for the camera and placing it on the mantelpiece above the fireplace.

"Good idea," Maddy said, wondering to herself if having these reminders of their past life may be a bad idea, considering the bittersweet pain it would inevitably conjure up. She pulled out the picture frames one by one, not even looking at them until she placed them on the shelf. One by one, she set up shop, a home away from home with pictures of her family in happier times.

"This is my favorite," Allie said.

Maddy looked over and saw the picture of her and Allie playing with a beagle puppy. Teddy. Their father lying on his back, laughing as the puppy and girls jumped and screamed around him.

"I remember that day," Maddy said.

"You always have the best memory."

"No, I mean, I remember specific details of that day. I remember us going to the pound to pick up Teddy. We saw an ad in the paper and cried and cried for Dad to go pick him up. Dad didn't want it. You know how he was. But we begged and pleaded, and he said no. But the next morning we woke up and there was this little puppy in our room. That's the kind of man Dad was."

Allie nodded, putting another picture of their father on the shelf. She looked as if she was about to cry. Maddy wanted to reach over and give her a hug, to let her know everything would be okay. Give her some kind of reassuring aphorism that maybe she herself didn't even believe, but then she stopped herself. She stopped herself when Allie's face suddenly contorted back to one of seriousness, as if she willed herself to overcome any emotion that would bring her down. A trait that she didn't want her to have. A practice she had done herself maybe all too well.

Maybe the pictures weren't a good idea. Maddy didn't bring any herself when she left home. Her sharp and detailed memories were always only a thought away. Now with these pictures on the mantel. All she had to do was *look*.

"I remember Teddy," Allie said. "Remember, he had this bark like a seal. Maybe we should get a dog."

"What kind?"

"A beagle! What else?"

"Would drive the neighbors crazy," Maddy shook her head. "Remember we're not in—"

The young women glanced at one another as the knock came at the door. Maddy silently cursed herself for forgetting to place a "no soliciting" sign above the doorbell. Intent on scrubbing the place and clearing out the cobwebs that had gathered while the place had sat empty, they were both dressed in scruffy clothing, their hair tied in scarfs, faces free of make-up.

"Who could that be?" Allie asked.

"We won't know unless we answer it," Maddy replied, laying down her duster and wiping her hands on her worn and faded jeans. She walked to the door, placing a smile on her face as she opened it.

The woman standing on the porch had blonde hair with sky blue streaks on the ends, looking the polar opposite of the sisters. Both Maddy and Allie had ivory white skin, dark brown eyes, and hair so inky black it looked like a river of molten lava as it cascaded down their backs. In contrast, the woman outside looked like sunshine and summer personified, honey blonde waves cascading down in a glorious waterfall, sparkling blue eyes, and skin that made Maddy think of the warm sand of a Californian beach. The woman held a large casserole dish in her hands.

"Hi, can I help you?" Maddy said, brightening her smile a little more, something she would see her mother do when she tried selling tickets to the church raffle.

"Hi," the woman breathed, her own smile lighting up her already glowing face. "I saw you move in the other day and could hardly wait to welcome you to the block. The welcome gift of food, well, it might seem a little corny," she said with an apologetic shrug, "but it's traditional and we genuinely think it can help. The last thing anyone has time for when trying to clean and unpack is cooking, so, here it is!"

She held out the casserole dish, practically presenting it to the sisters like an award. Maddy took it, taken aback by the weight for a moment and almost dropping it. "Thank you very much, that's really kind of you. Umm, would you like to come inside? I'm afraid we haven't..."

Maddy tailed off. The woman had stepped inside before she'd even got the invitation out, looking around her with interest. "I see you're doing a good job of cleaning the place up. It seems like forever since I've been in here."

She'd wandered off down the hallway, looking into rooms as she went. Maddy trotted after her until the two of them ended up in the kitchen and she was able to relieve herself of the heavy dish, laying it on the countertop. "You knew the previous occupant?"

"A married woman," the neighbor said. "Name was Patricia. She rented the place as a get away from her husband, and we'd have gatherings in here. You know, just the gals."

"Yeah, I got really lucky. Rents here are so high."

The woman shrugged. "This house hadn't been on the market for a long time. I heard you're working at the newspaper, Maddy."

Maddy was mildly startled that the woman knew her name. "I'm afraid you seem to have me at a disadvantage…"

"Oh gosh, where are my manners!" the blonde said with a laugh. "I'm so sorry. I'm just so used to everyone knowing everyone. I'm Serena, Serena Rockwell."

She held out a hand, which Maddy shook. "I'm Maddy, and this is my sister, Allie."

Allie had followed them in and stepped up to also shake Serena's hand, giving her a warm smile. "So, you've lived here all your life?"

"Yep, no other place I'd rather be. I own a store on Webster Street; it's enough to keep me busy."

"Oh, there were some really cool looking stores there. I noticed a few as we passed through town. Which one is yours?"

"Salt 'n' Sage is mine. You must drop in as soon as you have the chance."

"Is that a bakery or something?" Allie asked, frowning as she tried to recall seeing a bakery or a cake shop.

Serena laughed her tinkling laugh again. "No, it's more of a…well…let's just say a craft store, candles, holders, burners, oils, a lot of homemade herbal products and natural remedies. Trying to get certified to sell some pot, too. I'm kidding! A lot of the locals are very talented, and I sell a lot of their products for them. It's a way to all pitch in together for the good of the town. The store attracts customers, and the products keep them coming back."

"We'll be sure to drop in as soon as we're a little more organized," Maddy said, ready for this woman to be gone and to let them get on. "We've got an awful lot to do before Allie starts school."

"Of course," Serena looked at Maddy thoughtfully. "Well, I guess I should let you get on. Just wanted to do my part in welcoming you."

She gave them a bright smile and walked towards the door, opening it to let herself out, but turned to face the girls again before she did so. "Oh, forgive me. My sources only stretch so far." Serena gave them another one of her gentle laughs and a wink. "I don't know your surname."

"Oh, it's Stoner," Maddy said. She was surprised when Serena's eyes narrowed and hardened and her face took on a pinched look. She shivered, uncomfortable under the strength of the gaze that seemed to contain no small amount of displeasure. "Is something wrong?"

Serena seemed to remember herself, and the lines eased out as her face relaxed again. "Not at all," Serena said almost through gritted teeth. "Not at all. Hope you like my cooking."

With that, she was gone, closing the door behind her.

Maddy and Allie looked at one another, both their faces puzzled. Allie shrugged. "I'm not quite sure if that whole experience was really nice or really creepy."

"Me neither," Maddy agreed. "She did seem a bit strange."

"Well, we are in the Bay Area now. We're going to have to get used to strange."

~*~

Maddy got into reporting in part because she wanted to get rid of her shyness. The phone calls and in-person interviews really didn't alleviate her anxiety. But now, with her intuition bells ringing, she felt a helluva lot bolder as her cell phone trilled in her ear.

"Pick up," Maddy whispered. "Pick up, you old fart."

"Bill Mosley."

"Mr. Mosley?" Maddy said in her cheeriest voice. "It's Maddy from the paper."

"Right! Right! How's that hit piece coming?"

"Oh, well, that's the reason why I'm calling. I'm at a bit of an impasse. Curious if your wife ever rented a house on Haight Avenue in the Raven Heights district."

"Yeah, that was hers. She didn't sleep there though. Set it up as a meeting point for her Wicca club members."

"Do you remember anyone else that I could talk to about her? Someone involved that could get me access to that club?"

"Her name was Sabrina," Mosley said after a long pause. "No, that's the TV show. Um—"

"Serena?"

"Yeah," Mosley said. "That's her name. Real charmer that one. She could manipulate people like a puppeteer in a toy factory. Filled my wife's head full of that stuff. But we were at a point where I didn't care anymore."

"Can you be more specific? I mean, what kind of stuff?"

"The witchy-stuff," Mosley spat out, annoyed. "And it wasn't even that. The fact that it seemed like a cult. That she preyed on the vulnerable people in town. Like she had a sixth sense for someone she could manipulate. Middle-aged housewives like my wife. Wayward teenage girls."

"Teenage girls?" Maddy asked, images of Allie popping in her head.

"Yep. She was like a pied piper leading them on a trail to never, never land."

CHAPTER THREE

Three months into the school year and Maddy still hated her job. Still, she decided to stick it out for Allie's sake. Fall semester started for her, and she thought her younger sister had adjusted nicely to her new surroundings and if not, she should get a Meryl Streep award for being a good actress, as she seemed happy.

Pulling up outside the house, Maddy could hear the stereo blasting from her living room window.

All the leaves are brown,
And the sky is gray,

On the porch she saw Allie sitting on the swing set they'd just purchased for the porch, with a can of soda in hand. Another soda sat on the low coffee table in front of it. A girl sat with Allie, looking every bit the precocious teenager like her sister. She had long brown hair, tousled on top as if she had just gotten out of bed. Her halter top stopped just north of too much cleavage and she wore flip flops.

I've been for a walk,
On a winter's day,
If I didn't tell her,
I could leave today,
California dreamin'

"Dude," Maddy said, getting out of the car. "The music!"

"Sorry!" Allie said, taking the remote off the coffee table and pointing it at the window, lowering the volume.

Maddy wondered if this was the friend she'd spoken so much about recently. She had to work some long hours lately, and Allie had to fend for herself after school.

"Hey sis, this is Cheryl, my friend from school. Cheryl, this is my sister, Maddy."

"Hi, it's nice to finally meet you," Maddy said. "I've heard a lot about you."

"It's all lies," Cheryl rolled her eyes in a playful manner. She stood up tall, five foot ten, and tilted her head to look down at Maddy. "I heard you worked at the paper."

"Yeah," Maddy said. "How'd you guess?"

"A rumor in this household. I was thinking about going into journalism myself. I like snooping around other people's business."

"A bit more to it than that, but, yeah, it's a reporter's job to sometimes go beyond the boundaries."

"Do you like working there?"

"Yeah, it's the career I wanted. Although sometimes I struggle to find enough to write about. It can be pretty quiet around here."

"Well, one day, you might find out there's more going on than you might think," Cheryl said with a laugh.

Maddy smiled in response but made a mental note about Cheryl. What could a teenage girl know that she didn't? Beyond reporting on new crafts and the fetes and fairs in the local area, nothing much happened in the past few months. Outside of crime, there hadn't been much doing in Alameda. Before she had a chance to ask the girl about it, Cheryl rose to her feet.

"I should get going and leave you two to catch up on your day."

"You don't have to go on my account," Maddy said. "And you're welcome to stay for dinner."

Cheryl looked uncertain for a moment, then shook her head. "No, I'd best go. Thanks for the soda, Al. See you in Spanish class?"

"*Si,*" Allie waved her friend goodbye. "*Adios amiga.*"

With that, Cheryl was jogging down the short driveway, collecting a bike that was propped up against the hedgerow that Maddy hadn't noticed when she'd pulled up.

"Isn't she great?" Allie enthused.

"She seems nice, but Al?"

Allie shrugged. "It's what they all call me at school. I actually prefer it. Doesn't sound quite so 1980-ish, you know?"

"Sounds more tomboy-ish if anything."

"I like it."

"Okay, well, I'm still calling you Allie," Maddy agreed, feeling a little sad that her sister wasn't keen on the name their parents had given her but understanding her need to fit in. Maddy didn't like her given name either.

Suddenly she noticed something new on the coffee table in between the soda cans. "Oh hey, this is nice. Where did this come from?" she asked, picking up the lantern-shaped candle holder with a pretty lilac candle inside. She ran her finger across the four glass panels, crafted in brass with intricate metalwork inside. Is this meant to be ivy?"

"Yeah, it's cool, isn't it? I got it at Serena's shop."

That woman *again*. Allie couldn't seem to stop talking about her. Stopping by her shop after school seemed to have become a bit of habit for her. Maddy couldn't put her finger on why, but the idea made her slightly uneasy. Serena had been perfectly polite and the first to welcome them to the town, but for some reason, she always felt slightly uncomfortable when she thought about her. Her body language and vibe didn't quite match up with the superficially cheerful things that came out of her mouth. After Serena had gone that first day, Maddy had returned to the kitchen to inspect the casserole that had been presented to them as a welcome gift. It had looked delicious, and Maddy noted that it smelled as good as it looked.

But she threw it out anyway.

Afterwards, she'd felt confused and guilty, having no idea why she'd done it, and yet she'd also felt a great sense of relief. Her suspicions made no sense, and she was glad Allie hadn't seemed to remember about the gift and didn't ask about it. She wouldn't have had a clue how to explain what she'd done. Now, she didn't quite know what to say about Allie—*Al*, she thought with a smile—bringing home things from the woman's shop. "Was it expensive?"

"That's the best bit," Allie's eyes beamed. "She was in the middle of unpacking some boxes she'd had delivered. I helped, and she just gave it to me as a 'thank you,' said she'd had it and the candles laid aside for me anyway, as she thought I would love it. She's right of course; I do absolutely love it, and the candles smell heavenly. I've got one in my room too. Would you like one? They came in a box of six."

Maddy shook her head. "No, thank you for offering, but you keep them since you love them so much."

"Thanks, but I haven't even told you the best bit yet. She's offered me a job. A couple of hours after school every day and all day on Saturdays. The pay is better than what I'd be doing as a waitress back home, and I would get a staff discount!"

"You already took the job?"

"Well, I told her that I had to check with you," Allie raised her eyebrows. "Since you are my legal guardian? What do you think, Maddy, can I? It would be so much better than being on my feet all the time, waitressing somewhere. The money is better, and I'd be surrounded by all those beautiful things. Plus, I'd get to spend all that time with Serena. She's so interesting to talk to, knows so much about the town. Please tell me I can say yes?"

"No."

"No?"

"You don't want to do anything to jeopardize your college chances. You have a chance to go to Cal if you score high enough on the SAT. Why do something that is only going to take time away from your studies?"

"But I want to help out."

"Help who? Serena?"

"Help us," Addie said. "I had been talking to Serena about college, and I'm already thinking that staying in Alameda might be best for a few years. I can save, go to junior college, then transfer to Cal or someplace else."

"Let me think about it," Maddy said, hiding the fact that it hurt her feelings that Allie had been discussing her future education with Serena of all people.

"Fine."

"I'll get dinner ready," Maddy said, laying the candle down before walking inside the house.

~*~

Kelly paced around the roof of the newspaper building, waiting. She hated this part the most, the waiting. Serena would almost always give her assignments at the meeting place on Haight Avenue. Since when would they meet on the rooftop in the shivering cold?

"No progress?"

Kelly shuddered and spun around. She hated when Serena did that. Just popped in and out of thin air as if she had been there the whole time.

"I've been making her life miserable," Kelly smiled. "You know, teasing her. Mocking her. She'll crack—"

"And do what?" Serena hissed. "Kill herself?"

"I can't do the direct route—"

"Why not?"

"She has some kind of good luck charm around her neck," Kelly could feel her voice crack. Serena scared her; her eyes were like deep canyons from a distant planet. "It's like she has a protective spell around her."

"A protective spell?"

"A good luck charm or something," Kelly raised her hands in the air hopelessly. "I was going to loosen some bolts in her car, and then she caught me as I was headed toward her vehicle. I put poison in her pastry and watched her throw it out without even taking a bite."

"Jesus, you're incompetent."

"What? What was I supposed to do? Just walk up and shoot her?"

"You're supposed to kill her and make it look like an accident. Duh.'"

"This is the first time I've failed to do an assignment. Cut me some slack."

"I know you're not very brave," Serena lowered her voice, forcing Kelly to strain her ears just to hear her. "You put on an act. Sometimes I think you don't want to be part of things. Remember, we didn't choose this path. This path chose us."

"I understand that. I mean. We still have people after her, right?"

"You were the chosen person for the job."

"I tried everything, believe me."

"Maybe you should have tried befriending her first? Get her trust and then—"

"It was more fun to do things my way."

"You were supposed to do things MY WAY!" Serena blew hard; a supernatural gust of wind blasted from her lips and slammed into Kelly, sending her toppling over the building's ledge.

Serena casually walked over and looked down the five stories below, Kelly's body now a contorted mess on the pavement. A van pulled up alongside the body, and her minions quickly dragged Kelly's body into the vehicle. No witnesses and no mess except for the blood on the pavement.

~*~

Later that night, Maddy went for her routine jog. She would drive across the bridge to Bay Farm Island and jog along the trail there. A relatively affluent area, the trail had ample lighting, and she had no concerns about being a woman alone at such a late hour. Plus, at this time of night, she rarely encountered anyone. She liked the solitude, the idea that she could be all by herself, and not be burdened by anyone. The only sounds she listened to were the soft lapping of the lagoon waters and her running shoes on the pavement.

She passed a "DO NOT FEED THE SQUIRRELS" sign and increased her stride. Putting on her earbuds, she pressed play on a list of motivational music videos she had made on YouTube. Then she let her mind wander.

Maddy couldn't get over her sister's interest in Serena. In the last year, she'd tried to be much more than a sister—she'd tried to be mother, father, confidante, mentor, and friend. She'd thought she'd been doing a pretty good job, too, and perhaps she was upset about recent developments simply because they let her know that she hadn't been enough, that she'd failed her sister in some way.

Suddenly, her thoughts were interrupted by the realization that there was another set of footsteps echoing through the night. She turned the volume of the motivational music on her iPhone down, just to be sure that the running feet weren't her own. She felt a slight tremor of irrational fear and cursed herself for it. Still, she'd never encountered another jogger at this hour. She listened carefully. The footsteps were behind her, a ways back, but by the sound of it, they were gaining on her very fast. She resisted the urge to glance nervously over her shoulder, not wanting to show any sign of weakness. Instead, she increased her pace a little, knowing that only a half-mile up the road there was a turn off that would eventually lead onto another road that would let her head back to her car. It would be cutting her run short but a safe move; she had to get where there would be other people within hearing distance should she need them.

The footsteps behind her increased their pace.

Maddy sped up some more, now scared. Her hamstrings were getting tighter, and her knees began to feel sore after the pavement pounding. Maddy knew her limits and realized that she needed to start pacing herself. There were no houses nearby. Only the lagoon on the left and a densely wooded area that stood before a few abandoned corporate buildings.

No one could hear her scream if she needed help.

Before she knew it, even with her increase in pace, the footsteps were almost directly behind her. They were heavier than her own, and with the ease that they'd caught her, she made the assumption that they were male. That only increased her fear.

"Great night for a run."

She let out a small shriek as the deep voice spoke almost directly at her side. She glanced around, her eyes wide.

"I'm sorry. I didn't mean to startle you. I'd assumed you'd heard me coming up behind you."

The man in front of her screamed muscles and fitness. The lighting from the trail lamps exaggerated his chiseled features. He had shoulder-length, jet black hair. Square-jawed, he had a five o'clock shadow on olive skin. His eyes looked like pools of obsidian but Maddy sensed a kindness in them. On top of that he was tall, at least six foot one or two, broad-shouldered, and toned in his running outfit. He looked both gorgeous and dangerous at the same time. The way he held himself reminded her of a tiger on a nature show, graceful, relaxed, yet with the impression that he was ready to pounce at any second.

"I did...you didn't...I mean..."

A deep chuckle resonated through the night. "I understand, and once again, I'm sorry. My name's Kane, Kane Darkson."

"Kane?" Maddy asked, her voice betraying a sense of disbelief. "Darkson? Sounds like something out of a bad romance novel."

"And Stoner sounds like something out of a Cheech and Chong movie."

She stopped in her tracks. Now the hairs on the back of her neck were tingling and standing on end, and she felt the icy, cold fingers of fear run over her body. "How do you know my name?"

The man had stopped with her as if anticipating her move. That deep, low chuckle came once more. "You're in the paper. I read your byline every day. Your picture is in the—"

"Yeah, I know. Not a really good explanation—"

"You wrote about the park leagues the other day. Good article."

"Thanks."

"But they're called the Longfellow Tigers. Not the Longfellow Lions. There is the Lincoln Lions."

"Oh," Maddy said. "Right."

"I moved here a while ago," he replied with a shrug. "Only know all that because I was going to coach some flag football to pass the time."

"But now you pass the time by scaring people on the jogging trail?" Maddy said, raising an eyebrow as her voice dripped with sarcasm.

"I make a special effort on that," he gave her an easy grin and pointed at the row of townhomes in the distance. "You jog past my house most nights, and my curiosity was piqued."

Maddy regarded him, her fear easing enough to take him in properly for the first time. After all, if he had any intention of murdering her and dumping her body out here in the lagoon, then he'd probably have done it by now.

Cooling down, she shivered in the night cold.

"You're getting cold; we should start moving again."

He looked at her questioningly, and Maddy nodded. She would prefer him running beside her where she could keep an eye on him rather than wondering all the way back if he was behind her or watching her. They began to run again, keeping a slow, easy pace.

"So, what brought you to town?" Kane asked, increasing his pace to match her long strides.

"This and that, research mainly. I'm a writer, and what I'm currently working on led me here."

"Well, I can't see that there would be much to research here, so you probably won't be staying long."

"Actually, I'm sticking it out at the paper and will remain here for a while. This is exactly the type of place I need."

"It's got a small-town vibe," Kane chuckled. "At least on the surface."

What was it with people around here and weird, enigmatic sentences that made no sense? She couldn't think of a suitable response, so she fell silent. Before she knew it, they were back into town, the streets empty as they jogged through. She wondered if she should try to divert him away from her car but figured a serial killer would have made his move by now. A few more moments and they were nearing her driver side door. She wondered what would happen next as she slowed down and eventually came to a halt. "Well, this is me."

He nodded. "Maybe we could run together again sometime. We newcomers should stick together."

She wasn't sure what she thought of that, so she gave him a noncommittal response. "Maybe."

He frowned. "I'd really rather you run with me or not at all. I don't think it's safe for you to be out here alone."

His initial words had made her bristle, not being accustomed to being told what to do and taking exception to it immediately. "Goodnight," she said abruptly, turning and getting inside her car.

Once inside, she locked the door behind her, breathing a sigh of relief as she leaned her back against the seat. She had to admit that the encounter had rattled her. Once she'd steadied her breathing and her pulse had slowed, she started her car and shifted into drive. Glancing at her rearview mirror, she kept her eye on Kane for as long as she could.

The man stood frozen in place, boldly staring at her car.

She kept watching him in her rearview mirror until finally he shook his head, as if clearing it from a trance, and turned away, jogging off into the night.

CHAPTER FOUR

Maddy sat in her car outside Serena's store. Watching patrons go in and out of the store, she waited until she surmised that there weren't any more people inside. She wanted to confront Serena without any witness.

Confront, she thought. She hadn't confronted anyone since Tiffany Watson stole her calligraphy pen in fifth grade.

Serena emerged from the side door of her business and looked down the street. Maddy instinctively moved down in her seat, even though there would be no way Serena could see her from so far. She watched, as Serena seemed to be waiting for someone. A car pulled up alongside the road, and a long-haired man in his middle fifties stepped out. He had his gray hair in a ponytail and wore jeans that had blotches of paint on them. He handed a plastic bag to Serena, and she led him to the back of the store.

Seizing her opportunity, Maddy almost ran to the store. Once inside, she would be able to snoop around undetected to try and find out some information on this mysterious Serena.

She opened up the door, and a wind chime signaled her entry. Damn, so much for a surprise visit. Still, her guess had been right. No customers were inside.

Maddy looked up and down the aisle, spotting items that looked like they belonged on an occult website rather than a local crafts store. There were ouija boards, tarot cards, and tons of different kinds of crystals.

"Can I help you?"

Maddy turned around, startled. But she recognized the voice.

"Allie?" Maddy said. "What are you doing here?"

"I work here," Allie said, pointing to the name badge on her chest.

"But we agreed—"

"You said it was okay."

"No, I didn't. I said I'd have to think about it."

"Well," Allie waved her hands in the air. "I couldn't wait. She made me a job offer."

"So?"

"So, every girl at school wants to work here."

"Really?"

"Yeah, really," Serena's voice bellowed from behind.

Maddy spun around, seeing the smug look on her enemy's face. "I didn't give her permission to work here."

"S'okay," Serena said. "I filled out her work permit myself. Know someone at city hall. Easy peasy."

"But you didn't have my permission."

"You're not Dad," Allie spat out. "You can't tell me what I can and can't do."

"Listen, Allie."

"Allie!" Serena stepped in between them. "Can you get that shipment of candles in the back? And just give us a moment, please?"

Allie stood between the two women, unsure of whom to obey. Sucking air, she went to the store.

"I'm her legal guardian," Maddy hissed.

"I know," Serena smiled like a snake. "I know. You're taking the role of the parent and I know it's hard. But she's eighteen in only a few months. We talked about this. She can make her own decisions now."

"It isn't your place to—"

"I know, I know. But she's going to do what she's going to do. You can't stop her. I'll take her under my wing. Trust me, she's in good hands."

Maddy clenched her fists. She felt like punching Serena. Sure, the woman had maybe seven to ten years on her, but Maddy didn't recognize any kind of elderly authority she thought she might have.

A customer walked in the door, an elderly woman with a beaming smile.

"Now, if you'll excuse me," Serena said.

~*~

Maddy didn't sleep well that night. She dreamed of her childhood home, which now became a recurring nightmare. The vision started in the backyard. She felt as if she wanted to enter the home but couldn't. Instead, an irresistible force prevented her from going inside. Feeling that her parents were still inside the home, she walked around the house, trying to peek in the windows, but all of the curtains were drawn. She could hear the voice of her father behind the walls, calling her mother's name. She knew he would be on his easy chair, watching a college football game. Her mother would be in the kitchen, preparing dinner for the family. Visions of her childhood came like a kaleidoscope, fragmented like a jigsaw collage. Her heart pounded, not in fear, but out of sadness. Nostalgia for a life that once was and now could never be. Why didn't she cherish the time more? In the dream, her parents were alive. The dream felt like real life.

She woke up with tears in her eyes. She wanted to go back to sleep. To see her Mom and Dad again.

But now she had a job to do.

Seated in her car, Maddy double-checked that her purse contained her notebook, several pens, and her iPhone. Having satisfied herself that she had all she needed, she grabbed the map from the glove box. With her cellphone service so unreliable, she'd given up trying to use the GPS on her phone a long time ago and resorted to more old-fashioned but reliable methods of finding her way around her new area. Wherever she was assigned to go, she would do a recon mission a day ahead of time to get used to the lay of the land. Rolling down the window, she let the summer wind hit her face; it carried the seaweed scent of the bay, and the damp chill gave her a needed energy boost.

Today she was visiting a part of town she'd never heard of before and wanted to double-check her route. Her cellphone had been relegated to pretty much just being her camera when she needed to take photographs of events. It hadn't been made clear in her job transfer that working local news meant that she would also be doing her own photography and sometimes answering the main line. Not exactly hitting it out of the park when it came to her career.

Today would offer no solace. A local man would be celebrating his ninety-ninth birthday. Maddy thought of it as a somewhat noteworthy achievement. She wanted to take his picture and get out of there before he drooled on her new shoes.

But first, coffee. She entered the Starbucks that still had the Christmas decorations up. Maddy didn't like the surreal look of candy canes and Christmas tree stickers up on the wall. It reminded her of Christmas with her family. Times with Mom and Dad and presents under a tree.

A time long gone.

Now she had to deal with the green-haired barista manning the counter. The young woman handed a hot cup of coffee to a man who looked familiar.

Kane.

Gosh, how small was this town?

Her heart pounded. She wanted to turn back around and pretend she didn't see him.

"Maddy?"

Too late.

"Hi."

"Hi there," Kane said, sipping the frost away from his Frappuccino. "Pumpkin spice latte. A witch's brew."

"Sounds good," Maddy said, stepping to the counter.

"Would you care to join me?" Kane waved to an empty window seat.

"Um, sure," Maddy shrugged her shoulders. She had always been like that. Couldn't think of a lie fast enough in order to weasel out of a situation. And she just couldn't say no.

She ordered a caffè mocha and sat down across from Kane, who looked at her with attentive eyes.

"So," she said, her voice thin as she began to realize how handsome Kane's features were. "You never told me what kind of research you were doing here."

"Oh, a little bit of this and that. Mainly focusing on the history of the town."

"Interesting. Every town has a history."

"Yep," Kane said, sipping again from his cup. "How are you liking the town so far?"

"Interesting," Maddy laughed. "Only fly in the ointment is Allie. My sister and I have become a little distant lately."

"It's to be expected," Kane said in sympathy. "Happened with my little bro and me. We were close, then time goes on. I'm working. He's working. You know how it goes. Just important to see the fissure coming, you know? Make sure you go home tonight and give her a hug. Hold her tight. Tell her how much you love her."

"Wow," Maddy said. "Um, yeah. You're right."

"She's young?"

"Teenager."

"She's always with her friends now, right?"

"Ah, yeah," Maddy nodded. "Plus, her new job, which she really likes. I mean, she's not the typical teenager; she's happier and more animated than she's been since our folks died. But—"

"What?"

Maddy thought for a beat. She had given this man more information than he needed or even earned to hear. "I shouldn't burden you with my problems."

"I won't judge," Kane smiled in empathy. "Believe me, I have experience with difficult teens."

"That's the thing," Maddy felt a sudden spike in her trust for Kane. He spoke slow and confident; the timbre of his voice gave her a slight tingle. "She's not difficult. I just feel as if she's keeping something from me."

"They're all like that," Kane laughed, then turned serious. "And I'm not being dismissive. Teenagers today speak in a different code than we're used to."

"I sometimes feel that she's not telling me the truth," Maddy confessed. "And I feel powerless over her. I can't tell her to ditch her new friends or quit her job. I mean, I can, but how can I enforce it? I'm just the older sister."

"I wish I could help," Kane said. "But you're a smart woman. You should trust your hunches and go with your intuition. If you feel something is wrong, then something is."

"Thanks," Maddy looked at her watch. "I really should go. I have to interview a ninety-nine-year-old man for the paper."

"Where?"

"At the Ballena Lodge. The rest home on the other side of town."

"Stay safe," he tilted his cup of coffee at Maddy as she walked out of the door.

~*~

"He's having a really good day today," Katy Wilson told Maddy as she handed her a mug of coffee in the kitchen. "Most of Uncle's days are good days. There's only the odd time when he gets a little vague and distant. He's pretty much still as sharp as a tack, and his tongue can be just as sharp when he wants," she added with a laugh.

"That's good to hear," Maddy replied with a smile. "I never know which would be worst to live with, the mind going first or the body."

"I know what you mean, but he does okay on both scores, so we're pretty lucky. He's looking forward to meeting you, says a change of a face will be nice. He doesn't get out so much nowadays, so mostly he's stuck with me."

"Are there any specific subjects he likes to talk about? I've written up some questions to ask that I thought might be interesting to our readers, but mostly I'd like this to be fun for him."

"I'm pretty sure he'll lead you down any line of questioning that he wants," Katy said, grinning as a kettle of boiling water whistled urgently. "Lemme get his coffee and I'll introduce you both."

Matthew Wilson sat in his wheelchair, looking as frail as Maddy expected him to be. He raised his hand to her, gnarled with creases and cracks; it seemed abnormally large for a small man.

"Mister Wilson," Katy said, raising her voice. "This is Maddy from the newspaper. She wants to do a story on you."

The old man appraised Maddy for a moment. "I have a thing for faces. Beautiful faces. Please. Sit."

An hour and a half later, Maddy noticed that Matthew seemed to be getting tired but didn't want her to go. She felt guilty because she had to leave and he seemed appreciative that someone actually wanted to talk to him. She'd asked him questions, had some really great stuff on the changes to the town over the years, the characters that had lived there, and the newcomers that had come and gone. She also had some great shots of him with his birthday cake, banners and balloons, and sound bites from the other family and friends that had arrived or popped in to wish him a happy birthday. She had more than enough to put together a decent human interest article, but the man didn't seem to be nearly ready to let Maddy go yet.

"Sit with me and have some cake," the old man licked his cracked lips. "We might as well cut it and eat it instead of it sitting there looking pretty."

"Oh no, I really have taken up too much of your time."

"Yeah," the old man wheezed with teenage boy sarcasm. "Like I have tons of things to do today."

"Besides, you want to save your cake and not give it away to a practical stranger."

Matthew looked at her. "Stranger? What was your name again?"

"Maddy. Maddy Stoner."

The old man's face broke into a grin. "If you're a Stoner, then you're no stranger at all. I've known your family since I was a little boy. I knew you looked familiar; you have the look of your father about you. I have a thing for faces. Eyes. I could recognize him in you."

Maddy wasn't quite sure how to handle the moment. It was obvious that the man's mind was finally starting to wander after remaining clear all this time. Her mother and father were both from out of state and had met and married in Salem. She very much doubted her father had ever been down this way and certainly not for long enough to make friends and be remembered. Should she shatter his illusions or simply play along? She decided playing along would be best; she didn't want him getting upset on her account. "Is that right? You knew my family?"

"Oh yes, dear. Your father was born in my town, as was his father, and his father before him. Stoners have always been here. It was only when Helena was heavily pregnant with her first that Justin decided to leave and move to the city, and that's the first time there have been no Stoners here for a long while. That must have been you, my dear, and I'm so glad that you've come home."

Maddy stared at the old man, open-mouthed. Helena and Justin were her parents' names, but this couldn't be right. She realized Matthew was asking her a question. "I'm sorry, I beg your pardon?"

"Where about are you living?"

"Haight Avenue. Just off Webster."

"The Raven Heights neighborhood," he replied absently, still half-lost in his racing thoughts. "You can't live there. That's where it all started. That street is wicked. Evil lives there."

"Oh, it's quite sweet, really."

"No! It's no place for a Stoner to be. You must get out of there; it's not safe for you. They know the bloodline, you have to—"

"Hey, what's going on?" Katy asked, stepping into the room and rushing over to her agitated Uncle. "It's okay Uncle, everything's okay, hush now, everything's fine." Kneeling down in front of him, she glanced over her shoulder at Maddy. "I'm sorry, I think he's tired. If you've got everything you need?"

Maddy caught her meaning and immediately gathered her things. "I'll be on my way. I'm so sorry if anything I said upset him."

Katy gave her a terse smile.

"I'll see myself out."

Feeling a little deflated at how this had ended, Maddy began her drive home. She felt bad that Matthew had grown upset and it had put a damper on the day, as well the thought of writing up the article. However, what the old man had said held the much greater importance. It couldn't be true, could it? Her parents had always told her that they'd met at college in Salem and it was love at first sight. They'd also said that both sets of families were from out of state and they'd lost contact, which was why they were never in their lives. If what the old man said was right, then their parents had lied to them all their lives. The old man must have been mistaken or simply confused. Ninety-nine years old. His mind couldn't be all there.

But the reporter in Maddy wouldn't be denied. She made a U-turn and headed back to the town hall and library.

~*~

Allie sat at the far end of the park underneath a large pine tree. Wind whistled through, sending a few pine needles into her hair. She wiped them away, looking around herself. The solitariness of the park made her feel alone, like the night the sheriffs knocked at her door to tell her what happened to her parents.

Allie dribbled out the herbs in a circle just like Cheryl had said before placing the votive candle in the center. She lit the wick with a lighter she stole from one of the potheads in her ceramics class and later laughed to herself when he patted down his pockets looking for it.

"Okay," she muttered to herself, opening her spell book. "Let's get down to business."

Allie remembered what Cheryl had told her. To be wary of Kane and that he would be trouble for her and Maddy. Cheryl said this because Serena had told her so.

Allie closed her eyes and imagined both herself and Maddy standing together. To begin casting this spell of protection from Kane, she imagined them engulfed in huge white light—

"Fancy seeing you here," the deep voice came from behind her.

Allie spun around fast and stood halfway up.

Kane put his hands up in appeasement. "Just happened to be out for a jog."

"A jog?"

"I saw you from over there," Kane pointed to the trails behind the tree line. "Thought that was you."

"Yeah, well, I come here to think things through."

Kane looked at the ground and saw the herbs, candle, and crystal to the side. "Looks like you're casting a spell or something?"

"Yeah, what if I was?"

"No business of mine."

"Well, I'm casting a spell for you to get out of here."

"That'll probably work," Kane laughed. "But remember, black magic has a way of backfiring on its practitioners."

"What do you know about black magic?"

Kane reached down and picked up Allie's spell book. His face immediately turned to one of consternation. "I had a girlfriend once."

"Congratulations, playboy," Allie interrupted.

"She got into witchcraft," Kane thumbed through the book. "Started innocently enough until—"

Kane paused and took a deep breath; a haunted look came upon his eyes.

Allie couldn't tell if the memory caused him too much pain or if he thought her to be an unworthy audience.

"Let's just say that there were things she got involved in that consumed her," Kane looked Allie straight in the eye, his eyes like dark gems.

"Whatever," Allie said, taking the book out of Kane's hands. Kneeling down before her candles, she closed her eyes. "Great Goddess of Darkness and Night, remove this creeper out of my sight."

Opening her eyes, she looked back at where Kane had been standing with a sassy look on her face.

Only to find him gone without a sound.

~*~

Matthew sat at the end of his bed with his eyes closed. He used to enjoy the silence of the rest home, but now it simply unnerved him. He wanted someone to run down the halls, screaming and yelling. He wanted someone to do anything to show any kind of life.

"Knock, knock," Philip called out from the door.

He liked Philip, a young man who always greeted him with a cheerful personality.

"Look who's here," Philip said. "Your granddaughter!"

"Julie?" Matthew asked. He reached inside his pajama pocket and shakily put his glasses back on.

"I'll bring that to him," Julie said, taking a glass of hot water from Philip's hand. "He always liked my tea."

Julie walked over to the counter and dipped the tea bag into the cup. "Grandpa! How've you been?"

"Great," Matthew said. "Thank you so much for visiting."

"I know I don't visit enough," Julie said, handing the tea to the old man. "But when I do, I come with gifts."

"Thank you," Matthew cupped the hot tea with both hands. He curled his wrinkled lips and brought the cup to his mouth, slurping.

"How's that?"

"Good."

"Just like Mom used to make, right?"

"Sure," Matthew tilted his head at the young woman. "What brings you in?"

"A girl can't visit her grandfather," Julie exhaled. "Come on, let's go out and play bingo or something."

"No," Matthew said. "I'm fine. It's been a long day."

"Yeah," Julie said. "I heard you had company today?"

"I never have company," Matthew said matter-of-factly.

"Some cute reporter girl talked to you today—"

"Oh, her," Matthew took another sip of the tea. "Yeah. How has your Mom been?"

"Oh, you know Mom," Julie said. "She's fine. Said she'll come visit on Christmas."

"I'm old," Matthew spat. "But I don't have Alzheimer's. My daughter is dead. And it would be a cold day in hell when any of my grandchildren visit. So why don't you tell me who you are?"

A purple light flashed in front of the old man. He rubbed his eyes hard. In front of him stood another woman, a woman he recognized from years ago.

Serena Rockwell.

"I thought I warned you about talking to people," Serena snarled.

"Maybe I don't hear too well," the old man hissed, trying to stand up.

"No one is going to believe an old man's tales," Serena mocked. "Especially one going on and on about witches. But I've decided not to take any chances."

"They will, if I'm killed."

"If you're found murdered?" Serena shrugged her shoulders. "Then yeah, maybe."

"So, you won't kill me?" Matthew wheezed.

"I already have," Serena pointed at the cup of tea. "Good night, old man."

CHAPTER FIVE

Maddy didn't get home until eleven that night. She flipped on the light switch in the kitchen and saw a note on the countertop. Thirsty, she ignored the letter and headed straight for the fridge, popping open one of Allie's sugar drinks. Downing the soda, she set the kettle to boil and began sifting through her various tea bags in the drawer, settling on the "Peaceful Sleep" labeled green tea.

Then she finally picked up the note.

Allie wrote that she would be staying over at Cheryl's house. The news relieved her a bit. She now had a quiet house all to herself.

The staff at the library had been helpful, and she had full access to the newspaper archive room after hours. Her research left her shocked, dumbfounded, and in some ways a little hurt. Generations and generations of Stonehers lived in this area just as the old man had told her. This included her father and her mother, Helena Blackwood. She found records of their birth, as well as their high school graduation and yearbooks, which left her wondering why she never questioned or researched these facts to begin with. The old man didn't lie. Her parents did.

But why?

Dad had always been poor. Her mother hadn't been much better. Were they ashamed of their poverty?

Maybe they'd fallen out with the family and didn't want the girls in contact, so they had lied about them being out of state. Whatever explanation she came up with, it didn't seem likely or nearly enough to cover the magnitude of the lies. The stories about growing up in Salem—where they were supposedly respectively from, the schools they attended, where and when they graduated—had been fabrications. Maddy took a sip from the tea as her mind raced. Shaking her head, she knew she had to go out for a run. She did her best thinking on the trails.

It took less than ten minutes to throw on her jogging pants and stretch on the front porch. The late hour meant she'd be alone on the trails, but that suited her just fine. She set off, simply letting her mind drift, giving it a chance to work through everything on its own, trying to let her subconscious take the lead.

Her mind raced of dinner table conversations that were aborted when the subject of her parent's past came up. She did remember her father mentioning the fact that their last name Stoner had been abbreviated from Stoneher with an 'h.' He said to be proud and be sure to make up marijuana jokes to beat the smart alecks at their own game. Whenever the subject of grandparents came up, she remembered both Mom and Dad being tight-lipped. She did know that her parents loved both her and Allie deeply, so whatever the reason for not telling them the whole truth about their past, it had to be a good one. A reason to protect them.

But what if she didn't want to be protected?

A gust of cold wind hit her face, but Maddy had already begun to work up a sweat. She put her earbuds in and started to play some fast-driving grunge music for a beat, then shut it off. She had to focus, let the memories of her past coalesce into something that would make sense of her discovery.

She paid no attention to the route she took or how long she'd been running; she focused on her breathing and putting one foot in front of the other. She'd completely lost track of her location when a pair of lights up ahead caught her attention. Her interest piqued; she forgot her own issues for the moment and picked up her pace until she was on the asphalt right across from where she could see them. The trees were so dense she couldn't make out what she was looking at, no matter how much she tried to peer through them. She stepped off the pavement and onto the thick carpet of leaves.

Slowly, she made her way forward, the ground beneath her now pitch black and the light from the stars and moon waning the deeper into the field she went. She thought she heard the sound of distant music drifting on the breeze but couldn't be sure it wasn't just the sounds of the night playing tricks on her. The lights were definitely real though, and as she drew closer still, she realized she was looking at fires, one large one and several smaller ones. The larger fire, although the flames were flickering and dancing, was static. The smaller ones appeared to be moving. Having already adjusted to only the darkness penetrated by nothing but the silvery light of the moon, the brightness of them hurt her eyes. She had a feeling she should turn back and get out of there. She'd seen enough scary movies in her time to know that this would be the moment that the ominous music would begin.

"A satanic cult," she muttered to herself, trying to keep things light. "Or maybe a secret vampire club."

But what if they were a den of drug dealers that would hunt her down to protect their identity? What normal person would be up at this hour in the middle of nowhere? There was a high possibility that these were people up to no good, at the very least some teenage knuckleheads getting drunk or high. She scanned the teenagers for any sign of Allie.

She got close enough to hear voices, and she reached the edge of a clearing. In the center of it, a bonfire burned brightly, illuminating the area. She stared, trying to make sense of the goings-on. Several people were walking around the fire in a slow circle. They were robed, holding fiery torches aloft as they danced and dipped. She realized that what she heard earlier had not been music. They were chanting. Murmuring unintelligible words to the rhythmic pounding of a drum. Encased as they were in the blood-red robes with the large hoods, Maddy couldn't make out anything at all about the participants. Were they making a movie? She continued to watch, fascinated as the chanting grew louder and took on an air of frenetic urgency as the circle dance around the fire sped up. Their turning and dipping had a hypnotic, almost mystical quality. She fought a strange urge to come out from behind her tree and join them.

"So now you know."

The low, deep voice in her ear made her give a little shriek of surprise and fear. As the drummer looked over in her direction, trying to see through the tree line, a hand clamped over her mouth, and she was yanked down to the ground behind a tall shrub. "Be quiet, and don't move!"

Maddy gave an almost imperceptible nod, knowing that the strong fingers over her mouth would feel it. "Can I trust you to be quiet if I let go?"

She nodded again. Slowly, cautiously, the hand moved away from her mouth. She took a deep gasp of air, filling her deprived lungs. "Kane," she said in a low murmur. "What are you doing out here?"

He didn't have time to answer, for at that moment, the drumming stopped and they both turned their attention back to the clearing just in time to see most of the dancers drop to their knees. Only one remained standing. The burning torch and the other hand holding an item that Maddy couldn't quite make out, but glinted like steel in the firelight, were held aloft. One man held the torch high, and the drummer stepped forward to relieve him of it.

The drummer bowed her head, then tilted it back up abruptly, forcing the hood to drop, revealing the person's identity.

Serena Rockwell.

Maddy gasped. "What's *she* doing out in the woods in the dead of night?"

Kane's low and soft response sounded puzzled. "If I tell you, you have to believe me."

"I have no idea what to believe," she hissed. A part of her felt as if she were in another of her nightmares. She half-expected a dozen monsters to come out of nowhere and begin chasing her. "This place just keeps getting weirder and weirder. What the hell is going on out there?"

"If you don't know, then maybe you'd be better never knowing, except for the fact that your sister is getting heavily mixed up in it."

"My sister!"

"Shhhh! You don't want them to hear you. They'll be furious if they think someone is watching them and, believe me, you don't want to make them furious. Bad things happen to people who do that."

"What are you talking about? You sound like a lunatic but never mind that. Tell me, is my sister out there?"

"Not yet. She's exactly where she's supposed to be, over at Cheryl's house. She's safe for now, although I don't know for how much longer."

"How do you know that...never mind, I need to get her ass home."

Maddy made to rise, but Kane held her back. "Don't go off half-cocked. I agree that we should get out of here, but let's do it slowly and easily. I can't be responsible for what might happen if they find us here."

Kane led her out of the woodsy field, taking a less direct route than she had on the way in so that they emerged further down the road where they would be well out of sight of the clearing. Maddy looked at him. "I think you've got some serious explaining to do. And I'm going to get my sister."

He held her gaze even as they walked briskly through the dirt.

"I can't let you do that. If you do, they'll know that you know."

Maddy threw up her hands in exasperation. "I've already told you that I don't know anything! I don't even know what the hell that was back there, or what my sister's getting mixed up in, and I demand that you tell me right now!"

"Not out here. Let me come back to your place and I'll explain there."

She looked at the hard set of his face and knew there was no point in arguing the point any further. If she wanted answers, she was going to have to do what he said.

CHAPTER SIX

Maddy paced around the confines of her small kitchen. "So, let me see if I've got this straight, just so we're clear. You're saying that you're not a writer like you first told me but a witch hunter, and the reason you're here is because Alameda is a town full of powerful witches who are intent on gaining even more power and riches through any means possible? Am I right so far?"

"That's about it in a nutshell," Kane said. "But you left out how evil they are. These bitches are diabolical."

Maddy glowered at him. "I thought you were a nice guy, but you're really just a deluded whack job. You need to leave."

"Maddy, please," Kane raised his hands, pleading, "I know it sounds crazy. I know that. But you have to hear me out. You've still got no idea how involved you are in all this. I would say ask old man Matthew about it if you don't believe me but..."

Maddy looked at the pained expression on his face, and she felt tendrils of trepidation wrap themselves around her. "But what?"

"But he died this afternoon, just a few hours after you left him."

"No! But he was in such great health."

"Well, he was ninety-nine."

"What happened?"

"I'm afraid *you* happened, Maddy. You met him, and they knew that there was a whole helluva lot more he could have told you. He was a massive risk, so he was eliminated."

"Eliminated? What are you talking about now? Are you saying that these witches of Raven Heights murdered him?"

"That's exactly what I'm saying. Look, we're in a secret part of the town. A part where newcomers don't stay for very long. They escape or disappear. I know you think I'm being ridiculous. Or crazy. But I know what I'm talking about. I've watched them. Tracked them."

His expression and voice held such sincerity that Maddy flopped down at the kitchen table with a deep sigh. "You really believe everything you're saying, don't you?"

"I do, and so should you. Think about it, I mean, really think about it. How do you think Serena's shop can survive? Why is her shop even so popular? I bet too that she was the first person to greet you and that she brought you some food, not to mention that items from her shop have shown up in your house."

"How do you know all that?"

"Am I right?" his face looked serious. "Did you and your sister eat what she'd brought?"

"No. I don't know why, but I had a bad feeling about her, and even though there didn't seem a thing wrong with the food, I decided to throw it out."

"That's good to hear. Does she know that?"

"I would hope not! I would be so embarrassed at being that rude. I lied and told her it was great."

"That's even better. Right now, she thinks you don't suspect a thing, and that's the way you need to keep it until we figure out a way to get your sister away from them. She hasn't been initiated into the coven yet, but it won't be long. She knows, and she's studying with them, keen to join. Once she does, there's no getting out."

Witches, coven, initiated. The words jangled around Maddy's head as she tried to make sense of it, and she didn't even want to imagine what might have been in the food or in the herbal teas and candles that Allie kept bring back. The tea? She drank some. Maybe they were the cause of all of her recent nightmares and anxiety?

"But why the interest in Allie; what's so special about her?"

"The old man didn't tell you the whole story, did he?"

"Only that he thought he knew my parents and I didn't believe him anyway, thought he was just confused."

"He wasn't. Listen, I know this is going to sound really creepy but please don't freak out. Trust me, it was for your own good, and I had to know so that I could make my own decisions."

"What decisions, what are you going to tell me that'll freak me out?"

Kane sighed, not quite sure where to start. "I'm familiar with this area, kept an eye on it most of my life, but there was never any need for me to intervene before now. Everything was under control. Your family does come from around here, Maddy, no matter what you might have previously believed. They had a very special role here and when your parents left, they abandoned it, to the detriment of everyone."

"I can't believe my parents would do something that would harm anyone."

Kane shook his head. "I don't suppose that was intentional, more of a knee-jerk or gut reaction. I guess they didn't think through the massive consequences of them leaving."

"Why would they? What's the big deal of moving? People do that all the time."

"It was a massive deal for them and everyone left behind."

"You're straying into the realms of making no sense again. If it was a massive deal for them to leave and they were abandoning people that needed them, then why did they?"

"I can imagine only one reason. The role they had to take on when they came of age was a very dangerous one. It's not a life that's easy to live, and it's not one that's voluntary. My guess is that when your mother became pregnant, they decided to flee, to keep you safe and to prevent you from ever having to live the life you would be expected to if you stayed."

"Finally, you're saying something that might make sense, but what's this role that was so important?"

Kane reached across and took her hand. "This is probably going to come as a bit of a shock, but your family are witches too, Maddy. You come from a long line of powerful witches, more powerful even than the

Rockwells, but you've always been dedicated to the right side, the side of good and purity. Hundreds of years ago, you took upon yourselves the role of keeping the others in check and making sure they kept on the right path, suppressing their power and their magic so that they couldn't do harm. It's been a constant fight for generations, but when your parents fled, it left the whole place to the dark. The most powerful and accomplished witch quickly formed the Coven of The Ravens, took the role as High Priestess, and has been in charge ever since."

"Serena Rockwell."

"Exactly," Kane walked over to the window and peered through the slats of the blinds. "It wasn't long before she came to the attention of the witch hunters. I was given the task of looking into it all, discovering why the Rockwells had been able to take control. After discovering that the Stoners had left, I tracked them down. I watched you and your sister, needing to learn if your parents intended on instructing you and returning one day to take their rightful place and honor the role they'd been given. It was obvious that the answer was no."

Maddy drummed her fingers on the table, still having trouble taking this seriously. "Right, okay, that's the bit that I might have freaked out about then, the fact that you were spying on me and knew me before I even came here. Somehow, amongst everything else you're saying, a stalker seems like the least of my worries. Let me think. I know I don't want my sister mixed up in this—whatever it is—and I've had a bad feeling about Serena ever since I got here, but come on, witches? How much harm can dressing up and dancing around a fire really do? They don't really have any power; it's mostly hokum isn't it?"

Once again, he regarded her so intensely with his obsidian eyes that it made her feel as if he wasn't simply looking at her, but deep within her. Maddy turned her back to Kane. His gaze thrilled and frightened her.

"Don't ask me that question, ask yourself. I know who and what you are, even if you don't. I'd hoped that seeing the coven engaged in their rituals tonight might have triggered something, but obviously not. Look deep inside your own heart, your own soul, and ask that question again, Maddy."

The way he said her name and used it frequently made her tingle, his voice almost hypnotic. She found herself doing his bidding, opening her mind and heart, and asking the question again. She didn't find immediate enlightenment and understanding as she'd hoped, but she did feel *something*, a tiny whisper of a deep and buried knowledge that she couldn't quite grasp.

"So just how dangerous are they? I mean, Matthew was an old man. What happened to him could have happened at any time. What was his cause of death?"

"A massive stroke, but don't be fooled. Don't underestimate them. Did you never ask about the last reporter who worked for the paper?"

"It never occurred to me. I just assumed they had gotten a job at a bigger outlet and moved on, natural progression, you know?"

"He didn't. It was a guy called Pete Sanders, who owned the paper. He found out some things, started to poke around and delve deeper. He wasn't as careful as he should have been and attracted the wrong attention. When the coven found out how much he knew, they got rid of him. And Kelly was their woman, a plant if you will."

Once again, Maddy decided not to question but to go with it for now. "Then why take in an outsider to fill the position of a reporter? Why not use one of their own people to prevent it from happening all over again? There could only be so many reporters they could get rid of before someone started to notice."

He took a moment to answer, and when he did, his voice was quieter than she'd ever heard it before. "Think about it."

Frustrated and wanting the immediate gratification of clear answers, she had to force herself to do so. The idea that finally popped into her head caused her to gasp. She had to be wrong, didn't she? "It wasn't...I mean...is it because they wanted me, specifically me?"

"Yes," Kane nodded. I'm not going to sugarcoat it. I managed to find you, and it was only a matter of time before they did too. It was obvious to me that you knew nothing of your heritage, and it wouldn't have been hard for them to come to the same conclusion. The death of your parents gave them the perfect opening to orchestrate everything for you to move to the town with no interference or chance of you learning the truth before you got here."

"So, if my parents hadn't died, I wouldn't be here now?"

He looked at her with such sadness it tore at her heart. "If they'd watched you all of your lives, your parents' death might have always been inevitable."

Maddy stared at him for a moment, then shook her head, absolutely refusing to believe that their car accident had been anything other than that, a terrible accident. To even start to think otherwise would break her, and she'd taken long enough to recover from it as it was. Kane understood and moved on.

"There's no doubt that they orchestrated your move here. You got a job offer from LinkedIn, right? They came to you directly."

"That's right."

"Then they made your life hell, making your days intolerable, turning everyone against you, maybe even getting you into trouble with your superiors?"

"Things along those lines, yeah."

"Because they were witches," Kane said.

"Oh," Maddy rolled her eyes. "They were witches all right, but with a capital 'B.'"

"This isn't a laughing matter," Kane scolded. "If they'd placed some of their people around you, they know far more about you and have gone to greater lengths than I'd originally thought."

"But why? What do they want with us?"

"They're afraid of you. Your power. This struggle between the light and dark has been going on for centuries, and your ancestors always won out. You are stronger than they are. Can you imagine what they could achieve if they had that power on their side, merged with their own, the battle over and the forces united? A Stoner who knew their role would die before allowing it, but one ignorant of the whole situation is a different matter. Can you imagine being shown what you possess, being taught, guided, and mentored in its discovery and development, how honored, special, and grateful you would feel, how it would so easily warm you to those doing the guiding?"

"Allie!"

"Yes. They've obviously found you to be a little less easy and, for now, are concentrating their efforts on your younger and more easily led sister. She's starting to practice the craft herself. She has no abilities yet. But when she does. Jesus. I have no doubt that once she's initiated and has pledged her allegiance to their coven, they will, in turn, use her to convert you also."

Maddy leaped to her feet. "Then we have to get her away from them right now!"

"How do you propose to do that? I take it I'm right in saying that she's become distant from you since moving here, that you are no longer her entire world, her confidante, her friend?"

"That's all true," Maddy said, her voice filled with sadness. "But I'm still her legal guardian. I could force her to come home."

"And then what? Stop her going to school, force her to give up the job she loves, lock her in her room? You'll only create a greater rift and give them ammunition for them to turn her against you if you won't comply with their wishes. You'll end up pushing her more towards them. Is that what you want?"

"Of course not." Maddy sat back down, worry and defeat on her face. "So, what exactly do we do?"

"I do what I always intended to do, what I came here to do. I kill the coven."

CHAPTER SEVEN

Maddy stared at Kane in horror, his last words seeming to hang in the air between them as if they had physical presence.

"Did you just say 'kill'?" she whispered.

"I'm a witch hunter, Maddy. It's what I do. What else did you expect?"

Maddy shook her head slowly, unable to believe what she was hearing. "I don't know what to expect. Duh. I mean, you can't just kill people."

"Not normal people, no, but these aren't normal people. Black magic witches will stop at nothing, use whatever means they deem fit, to achieve their objective, remove anyone who stands in their way, and congratulate themselves on it rather than lose sleep over it. I've been watching them for a long time, in the same way as I've been watching you. I know them, and just as you were born to be what you are, I was born to be what I am. I can no more change my nature than they can or you can. I must do what is right by the codes of morals and ethics that I was born with as have generations before me."

Maddy was still shaking her head, thinking of the residents of the town. "You'd wipe out everyone just like that, without hardly a second thought?"

"Everyone involved with the malevolent practices, yes. It's not quite the whole town, and there are many just on the fringes, not so deeply involved that they couldn't be persuaded to work on the right side once the coven is gone."

"That doesn't make it any better. Even the loss of one human life is too much. And tell me, Kane, if your job is to kill witches, where exactly does that leave me if I am what you say I am? Am I next on the list?"

"My duty is to destroy those who choose to walk on the darkened path or use their power for evil instead of good. If you ever chose that way, then yes, you would be next on my list."

"Really?"

"But to be honest," Kane said, "I'd hesitate."

Maddy was taken aback by the brutal honesty but appreciated it, nonetheless.

"Well, I'm glad that I'm on the right side of things."

"I'm the least of your worries, trust me."

"Promise me you won't hurt Allie," she looked at him with piercing eyes.

"I'll make that promise for now, since she's uninitiated and I still believe she could break free of them. I can't make any such promise for the future, though. She would be very hard to deal with, not to mention the damage she could do to me and a lot of other innocents."

"Okay, it's probably the best I'm going to get, so I'll take it for now. I can't stand aside and let you kill them all though. There has to be another way; there just has to be."

"There is."

"Well, why didn't you say so?"

"Because I don't know if you're going to like it any better."

"Try me."

"You have to fight the coven, fight them and win, put them back in their place as your ancestors did, and keep them there. You have to reclaim your heritage and take over the role your parents never wanted you to have."

"How long have I got to think about it all?"

"I would say they'll plan your sister's initiation into the coven for the night of the summer solstice, as it's such a powerful time. That gives you roughly a month."

"A month! I can't do this in a month."

"You're a writer. You should be used to short deadlines."

"This isn't a damn news story!" Maddy angrily ran her fingers through her hair, exasperated. "This has all just been dumped on me; I don't know anything about this world!"

"Think," Kane said. "You're being negative. You're a positive witch. The good witch."

"Okay, fine. I mean, with you helping me—"

"I'm afraid you're mistaken," Kane said. "I won't be able to help at all, not if we do this your way. I'm a witch hunter, not a witch. My abilities are very different. I don't have any magic or power."

"Fair enough," Maddy stood up and began pacing again. "But you've studied them all your life, know things about how they think, how they work. You must have studied witchcraft as part of all that, at least to a certain extent, even if just to understand what you're up against?"

Kane nodded, conceding the point.

Maddy grinned. "Then you *can* help me. Knowledge truly is power. I should know, I'm a journalist."

~*~

"Just let go of logic and rational thought, Maddy, just feel it happening and let it happen."

Maddy tried again, concentrating with everything she had. Nothing happened. She dropped her head onto the table. "It's no use," she wailed, her tone laden with despair. "I can't do this. You're wrong. I'm not a damn super witch."

"You are, you're just trying too hard. You just have to connect with what's inside of you."

"You sound like some new age YouTuber."

"It'll come; it might just take some time."

"Time! We've been at this for ten days now. Time is the one thing we're running out of, and fast."

Even Kane looked concerned. "I know, I know," he muttered. "But I've been keeping an eye on the coven, and everything's pretty settled there. They've been watching you, but since you haven't gone snooping into anything since that day you met Matthew and have been acting normally, they're content to leave their original plan in place. They'll carry on watching you though, so try not to do anything that'll arouse their suspicions in the meantime."

"Won't they question how much time you've been spending with me?"

"They don't know who I am, and it just looks like a natural progression of the relationship we were building before. Besides, I'm pretty good at coming and going unseen when I want to be and making sure I'm seen when I do. You don't have to worry about me."

"What about Allie?"

"Just as I thought, the plans are in place for the solstice. Provided we keep them in the dark, that won't change."

Maddy stared at the dinner candle on the table she'd been trying to light without the aid of matches, thinking that she was the one that was going to make their whole plan fall apart if she couldn't get to grips with this. A pile of ancient-looking books was scattered around on the table beside it. Kane had brought them, telling her they were a small sample of his own education, gathered by his family as well as himself. They started with one of the easiest spells, a starting place for all witches to begin harnessing their power and experimenting with it. In her case, the wick remained pale and waxy, as cold and unlit as the magic within her.

This was just one of the simple spells they'd worked with over the past ten days, trying every different type of magic Kane could think of while he tutored her, trying to find that one thing that would allow her to reach inside herself and awaken it permanently. Nothing had worked.

"Why don't we get out of here," Kane said. "Maybe being closer to nature will help."

"At this stage, I'll try anything."

Kane drove them out of town and headed deep into the countryside. Finally, he drove off-road into a secluded spot and came to a halt, satisfied that the car wouldn't be easily spotted from the road. "Come on."

Maddy followed without a word as they tramped into the woods. She had no idea what Kane had planned for her, but she hoped it worked this time. All those lives depended on her, including her sister's. Finally, Kane stopped and turned towards her. "Go stand over there and focus on that tree."

She did as she was instructed. "Okay, so what do you want me to try?"

"I don't want you to try anything. I want you to die."

Maddy jumped and stared at Kane. For the first time, his handsome face looked ugly, twisted into a mocking sneer, his eyes blazing with hatred.

"But...but you said—"

"Whatever I said, I lied. You're a witch, the bane of my life, and a plague amongst the human race. I don't suffer witches gladly. You all need to be eradicated from the face of the earth."

His voice dripped with venom and echoed around the woods. It was as if he'd been infused with some ancient and righteous power. She could feel strength, and also hatred, radiating from him. Face pale in the darkness, her knees trembling, she began to back up. She wanted to plead and beg for her life but knew it would be pointless. She had to run. If she failed, she would die out here in the woods tonight. She'd almost reached the thick crop of trees she remembered passing only moments ago, where she had intended to make a run for it, when Kane sprung.

Maddy let out a scream, seeing his face screwed up in a vicious snarl and something silvery and wicked-looking glinting in the pale light of the moon. Instinctively, she threw up her hand to protect her face. It started as a small tingle deep in the pit of her stomach that grew and grew until she felt her tummy might explode at any minute. It was only a fraction of a second, but, to her, it felt like an age, and just when she couldn't stand the strange zinging sensation and the heat that was building up along with it any longer, her arms stiffened in front of her, fingers raised to the sky, palms firm and strong. She felt that sensation leaving her as if shooting out from her hands.

There was nothing to see, but suddenly Kane was flying backwards through the air. He landed heavily on his back, his head inches from hitting a sturdy trunk. Instead of making a run for it, Maddy let out a growl low in her throat and advanced on him. "All right, witch hunter, let's see you take down this witch! I won't be going without a fight!"

She loomed over him and her palms started to itch, desperate to release the power.

"Stop," Kane said, laughing. "Damn, you're strong!"

Maddy looked at him, confused.

Finally, he managed to control himself enough and get enough breath to talk. "Well, that certainly woke you up, didn't it?"

It took Maddy a moment before she realized that Kane had never been a threat. "Wait, so you weren't really trying to kill me?"

"May I get up?"

Maddy realized she was still holding her hands, palms down, over Kane. She hesitated a little longer, not sure what was genuine and what wasn't anymore. She decided she would back off a little but still be prepared to strike.

Kane rose slow and easy, keeping his hands up in the recognized surrender gesture. "Steady, Maddy. I can explain if you'll let me."

She gave him a nod of consent but remained on her guard.

"It seemed like the only way. You've been trying so hard and getting nowhere. I know this has been so hard for you to accept, and I think a large part of you still didn't really believe it and it was blocking you. Putting you in serious danger to see if it would trigger your natural instincts seemed like a plan. I'm sorry I had to frighten you. I saw it as the only way."

He seemed so sincere that Maddy couldn't help but begin to relax. He looked like the same old Kane again, the man she knew and was getting to like—a lot. Anyway, she suddenly felt more aware of everything, the sights and sounds around her as well as her gut instincts, and they were saying that he was telling the truth. It was as if she had suddenly woken up from a long, deep sleep, or if she had only ever been part of a whole before, a large part of her missing. It certainly wasn't missing any longer. She dropped her arms to her sides. "There really wasn't any other way?"

"None that I could think of that would work as effectively, and I was pretty sure it would work. No self-respecting witch would just stand by and be killed by a witch hunter without putting up one heck of a fight, and to do that, they'd use their magic. If I'd had the time, I would have called upon someone else, set up something elaborate. I'd have rather it not been me, as the last thing I wanted to do was damage the bond of trust we have between us, but with things as urgent as they are, it just wouldn't have been possible. It had to be me, no matter the consequences. The only thing that mattered was whether it worked or not."

"Well, it seems to have done that," Maddy said, staring at her palms in amazement as everything that had just happened began to sink in. "I really am a witch, aren't I?"

"You certainly are," Kane replied with a grin. "Now that you know it, we've got a lot of work to do, so we'd better get on with it."

CHAPTER EIGHT

Maddy glanced at the clock for the hundredth time that day. It was finally the day of the solstice, and everything that she and Kane had been working towards would be put into place that night. She'd worked non-stop on learning, developing, and honing her skills during every possible moment while trying to keep her routine as normal as possible. For the first time, she was glad that Allie was spending less and less time at home. Ever since that night in the woods, it was as if floodgates had opened. Working with Kane gave her strength she didn't know she had, but she still felt terrified of the night to come.

Kane had said he would enlist as much help as he could, although he warned her it wouldn't be very much by the time he narrowed it down to those that would be on their side, those that wouldn't double-cross them, those that wouldn't break if put under pressure, and those that wouldn't be too scared to come. It wouldn't leave him with much of a list. They also wouldn't know how many would arrive until the last minute since strangers in town would arouse suspicion. The last thing they'd wanted was for the coven to bring their plans forward.

Their own plan was that with her in charge, she and whoever arrived to help, if anyone, would wait until the Coven of the Ravens had carried out their initial dance where they summoned and called up their power within, then, before they went any further with their rituals that night, they would step forward from the shadows and bind all that power. Kane had assured her that it was within her capabilities.

"You were born to do this," he said, the words branding themselves into her memory. "It was your destiny. It was always your destiny."

She chanted the words inwardly as if they were a mantra, hoping they would give her both strength and courage. She wished her parents were here to help and guide her, but she had Allie to think about. She wanted her younger sister back by her side because without her, she felt so alone.

You have Kane, and whoever else turns up, she reminded herself firmly. As grateful as she was, she was so scared that it wouldn't be enough. So much sat upon her shoulders, so many lives, including that of her sister. She fully understood now that if she failed, Kane wouldn't hesitate to wipe them all out without a second thought. She simply couldn't let it happen.

She glanced at the clock once more, disappointed to see that less than ten minutes had passed since she last looked. It was just after 4 p.m. She wondered if she could cry off early, pleading a headache or some other malady. She was certain that Ken would let her go, but according to Kane, Ken belonged to them. If she left early, it could possibly tip him off. She'd just have to wait it out, act as if it were another day at the office. She might as well do some writing.

~*~

In Maddy's kitchen, just as dusk was falling, Kane handed her a wrapped package. "Here, I thought this might help."

"What is it?" She took the gift, a puzzled and nervous smile on her face.

"Open it."

Maddy rummaged in the drawer for the scissors and sat down at the table with the large, square package. She cut the string and removed the brown paper, revealing a strong, white cardboard box similar to a shoebox but larger. She opened the lid, the contents revealed to her not immediately shedding any enlightenment on the nature of the gift. A collection of items lay nestled there. For the moment she ignored them, her attention drawn to a large, ancient-looking tome that rested on the bottom. She pulled it out carefully.

The feel of the cover of the book beneath her fingers felt like leather, the color a deep, slate grey. Symbols and pictorial references embossed on the front were recognizable to her. She ran her finger over them—a pentagram, witches' runes, a depiction of Diana the Huntress, one of Cernunnos the Horned God.

"It's beautiful," she murmured, surprised at her own thought. Only a few weeks ago she would have found such a thing strange and frightening.

"Open it."

She opened the cover, revealing the first sheet of the yellowed, parchment style paper inside. Looking down at the writing, it looked as if it were completed centuries ago with a fountain pen. She read the first line aloud hesitantly, at first struggling with the ornate cursive. "Here within lies the pages of the Book of Shadows of the Stoneher family and their blood descendants. State your name for the records."

Stoneher! She let out a gasp, her eyes darting to nearly the bottom of the page, to the last name of the list. There it was. Justin Stoneher—her father. Unshed tears pricked at her eyes. She blinked them back, not daring to let them fall lest they smudged the ink below her. She looked at Kane, her face showing her inability to find any words that would come close to suitable.

"I made sure I was the one to collect everything after their deaths," he said, nodding as if he understood her emotion. "A Book of Shadows in the wrong hands can be very dangerous, especially from such a powerful bloodline. It was imperative that no one from the Coven of the Ravens got their hands on these items. I've also brought your mother's. The Blackwood line goes back almost as far in the area, and the two families were always aligned and united in their task, although the bloodlines were never combined until you and your sister came long. It makes you both very special, and I'm not surprised so much effort has gone into trying to initiate one or both of you into the coven. If they succeed, there will be no stopping them. It'll be the most powerful coven ever in existence. It's imperative we don't let that happen. I thought perhaps seeing this tonight might show you the magnitude of your heritage, maybe even let you draw strength from the energy you can feel coursing through these items still. That's your family's energy, including your father's. I'll leave you alone with it for a few moments while I fetch your mother's things in."

Maddy gave him a grateful smile and immersed herself back into the pages of script that went back for generations. She was amazed to find the binding spell that she'd spent the last few weeks memorizing in there, stunned to realize it had been the one used to bind the black magic of the Rockwells for decades. Kane must have copied it from the book for her, saving showing her these things for this very moment. The knowledge that she was using the same spell as generations before her gave her a certain amount of confidence she'd been lacking before. If she couldn't have it in herself, she could certainly have it in the ancient words of her ancestors. By the time Kane returned and they'd looked through both boxes and he'd explained all the items to her, she realized full dark had fallen and it was time to go. He'd kept her mind off it until the last moment.

****

"Are there any others coming?" Maddy asked as she sat in the passenger seat of Kane's car.

"I could only find three that were willing to go up against Serena Rockwell and the Coven of the Ravens, but don't let that worry you. They're only there to support you and watch your back. You could do this alone if you had to."

Maddy didn't argue with him, although she very much doubted his words. This wasn't a time for negativity. She needed to accept his faith in her and find it within herself. "I take it we're meeting them somewhere?"

"Yes. They're meeting us in the woods. I gave them a specific set of coordinates, and they all have a copy of the spell." He reached over and gave her hand a quick squeeze. "Everything's going to be fine, Maddy; this is going to work."

She said nothing more, remaining silent for the rest of the journey, lost in her own thoughts. When they arrived, Kane took great care to hide the car before leading her confidently through the dense, dark woods. He stopped and let out a whistle. One man and two women appeared from the shadows, as if from out of nowhere. Kane introduced them by first name only—John, Sarah, and Amanda.

John, a bespectacled man in his mid-sixties, stepped forward with a bright smile.

"An honor, Madam, an honor," John said, shaking her hand. "My wife, Amanda."

Amanda looked to be about ten years younger than John. No more than five feet tall with her white hair braided down in a ponytail that extended down to her buttock. She smiled at Maddy but said nothing as she shook her hand.

"I'm Sarah," the youngest of the three came forward. She looked no older than thirty and spoke with a husky voice. "I can't believe I'm meeting a Stoneher. A real-life Stoneher."

"We're here to help her,'" John scolded. "Not be her fan."

"But how can we not?" Sarah said. "Helping a Stoneher would be the highest honor. Your father, your grandfather. They mean so much to us."

"Thank you," Maddy felt a prickle of tears brim her eyes but she pushed them aside.

"It's time to go," Kane said. "The bonfire's lit."

They turned to look, seeing the distant glow of light from a blazing fire. They looked at each other once more, sharing a moment, needing no words. In silence, they followed Kane through the woods.

CHAPTER NINE

Maddy felt her heart race in fear as the circle dance began to speed up.

"We have to split up," Kane said. "Each of you will take a different point on the cardinal star."

They walked through the woods, slowly coming upon the dancing coven.

"The four corners are points of natural energy, the watchtowers. Each has a representation of the element that is tied to each point: fire, water, earth, or air. Maddy, I want you to approach from the East. You're the guardian of fire. Go."

Maddy walked forward in stealth, carrying her father's athame, a ceremonial knife which had the symbol of fire on its handle.

Arriving a short distance away and halting behind a thick tree trunk, Maddy almost lost concentration and dropped the mild masking spell she was using to keep her presence concealed from the coven. The fire itself was almost three times the size of the one she'd seen the first night. There were more people this time, four drummers in a line off to the side, a large circle of about thirty in an outer circle, robed and hands joined as they danced and spun. Inside that outer circle was another circle, thirteen people, all naked, their skin glistening in the lick of flames. *Skyclad*, Maddy thought, able to bring the correct term to mind. In the middle of it all were two young girls, holding hands and giggling as they watched the dance go on around them. They were robed, but their robes weren't belted, falling open and moving slightly in the soft breeze.

Allie and Cheryl.

Their eyes sparkled in the firelight, their cheeks flushed. It made Maddy feel sick, then angry. These poor innocents, no idea what they were about to tie themselves to, no idea what they were committing to or what the coven would have them become.

She knew that those on the outskirts would be the least powerful, the least committed, perhaps not even sworn to the coven itself, only following Serena, maybe not even voluntarily. They were the ones she could ignore unless they caused her problems. The ones she had to focus on were the inner circle, the thirteen key members that made up the coven true, the most powerful, the most devoted. Those were her targets, and she knew the others would know it too. She tried to push aside all the confusion and disgust that flooded her mind on seeing her sister here and focus on the task at hand. They had their queue to act upon and all she could do now was wait.

The drumming, the chanting, and the spinning sped up and began to make Maddy dizzy. At the same time, it stirred her soul and the desire to join in was almost overwhelming. This drawing down of power was in her blood; it was part of her, and when this was over and if she was still around, she intended to fully embrace it. Suddenly the drums halted, the spinning came to an abrupt end and the outer circle all fell to their knees, overwhelmed by the energy that even Maddy from her slight distance could feel humming in the air. It made her entire body tingle and buzz as if receiving a mild electric shock. She was so entranced by it that she almost forgot the dance coming to an end was their cue. As Serena Rockwell—skyclad with her long blond hair flowing around her shoulders, her head crowned with a tiara displaying the triple goddess symbol, eyes closed, a smile upon her lips—held a silver chalice up to the sky with one hand and began to call out a blessing upon the liquid within it.

Maddy knew her cue.

"Guardian of the watchtower to the east," she chanted. "Assist and protect me."

As if choreographed, the four all stepped forward at the same time, chanting the mystical words that would allow them to harness the power of Mother Nature herself, closing in on the coven, tightening the circle around them. She couldn't see Kane, but she could sense him close by. She saw Serena's eyes snap open, the slight confusion on her beautiful face turning to hatred mixed with shock as she saw Maddy approaching.

Her eyes flicked down to the athame in Maddy's hand, and understanding flooded her expression. She sneered, dropping the chalice and raising both hands in Maddy's direction. The battle was about to begin.

"Maddy, what are you doing here?"

Maddy ignored the squeal of dismay from her sister who hurriedly tied up her robe. She immediately switched to the words of the binding spell, gratified to hear the other three voices join hers. None of them had faltered yet, despite the rest of the coven turning to see what was happening and rapidly rearranging themselves in a tight circle around their high priestess. Maddy raised her voice, chanting the spell louder, the four voices perfectly attuned, creating a beautiful chorus that echoed through the night.

"Take her down."

Serena's voice was no more than a hiss, but Maddy heard it, nonetheless. Kane had warned her about this and had her working on deflection and protection spells in case she came under attack before the binding spell had taken full effect. She braced herself, ready for whatever was to come, her mouth still forming the words of the binding spell, while in her mind, she recited her words of protection. She had no idea who threw what, but only seconds later she felt a jolt. It wasn't that powerful, but it was an unfamiliar and unusual sensation that made her stumble only a little. She laughed. Either Kane was right and they were no match for a Stoneher, or the binding spell was already weakening them considerably. As they advanced to within a few feet of the coven, she felt several more of the jolts, but she didn't show any outward sign of them connecting, and they were already becoming weaker.

As soon as they reached the required distance, all still holding their four quarters, they moved on to the second and final part of the spell. As the coven began to look more panicked, Maddy realized that the jolts had stopped, that she wasn't even feeling the slightest tickle as they frantically tried to cast spells of harm upon her. Nearly all those from the outer circle had scattered, and now some of the inner circle made to follow suit. It looked as if Cheryl and Allie had also joined those that had fled, as Maddy couldn't see them anymore.

"Stop!" Serena cried. "Where do you think you're going, you sniveling bunch of cowards? Stand and fight!"

"She's bound our power," one man whined. "I've got nothing."

"So, you think you're helpless? Fight with your bodies, you fools."

Some shook their heads, deciding instead to take to their heels and make a run for it, thinking that their reign of power was nearly over and they'd be at the mercy of the Stoneher clan once more when this night was done. Three obeyed Serena, turning to fling themselves at Maddy, knocking her to the ground, and pinning her there, everything happening too fast for her to prevent it. One of them bashed her hand repeatedly against the ground until the athame fell from her grip.

Maddy struggled and fought, having been too taken aback to keep up the protection spell in her head, although she continued to chant the final part of the spell that would hopefully bind Serena's power for good. One of her adversaries tried to place a hand across her mouth, but Maddy bit at it, causing the woman to squeal and draw back. The man leaped on her, sitting astride her, compressing her chest while pinning her arms. She tried to kick but felt her ankles being restrained.

"Grab this arm," he snarled.

The woman that had tried to cover her mouth grabbed Maddy's left arm, and the man let go, raising his fist ready to strike her. One moment he was there, the next moment Maddy felt his weight lift from her as he was yanked off to the side, crying out. Amanda stood there, her posture menacing, her face steely. She raised her wand, representing air. The man whimpered and scrambled to his feet, running off and disappearing beyond the tree line. Seeing that she was free on one side, the woman holding her other arm let go and also fled. Maddy easily managed to dislodge the solitary remaining woman holding her ankles and soon had the athame in her hand again as she stood side by side with Amanda. Both of them raised their sacred items in the direction of the woman. Still on her hands and knees, staring at them wide-eyed, she crawled backwards, gaining some distance between them before she pushed herself to her feet and turned, running back to Serena and flinging herself behind her for protection.

"Thank you," Maddy said to Amanda. "I don't know what I would have done without your help. They took me too much by surprise, but you do realize that we've stopped the binding spell and you've broken the corners?"

Amanda's jaw dropped open, and a hand flew to cover it, only realizing what she'd done in retrospect. They both heard the sound of maniacal laughter from the direction of the fire.

"Amateurs! You've ruined your own spell, and I didn't even have to lift a finger. You'll never be able to start over and bind me now. And you thought you were good enough to go up against me, a Rockwell, the High Priestess of the Coven of the Ravens!"

Thunder roared and lightning split the air as Serena held up her hands to the night sky. "Time to feel the true power of a real witch. Prepare to meet your parents again in hell, Stoneher."

Just as Maddy flung Amanda away from her to remove her from the firing line of whatever Serena was about to unleash, knowing that years of being the leader of such a potent coven and so worshiped by the members had infused her with a frightening amount of power that she would be helpless against, a figure appeared from the side of the bonfire.

Jet black hair gleamed and shone, obsidian eyes burning with an intensity brighter than the flames themselves. Wicked steel glinted in his hand. Maddy could feel the strength of his presence, felt it radiating through the air, different from anything she'd felt from the witches both good and evil, but equally potent. He was like some terrible, dark, avenging angel. Knowing his intent, she opened her mouth to scream at him, to tell him to stop, even if it meant the loss of her own life.

She was too late.

In one swift, practiced move Kane slipped behind Serena, raising the long blade of his dagger and thrusting it through from behind. Blood exploded from her chest and mouth as her heart burst, pierced by the deadly witch hunter's steel. For one terrible moment the scene was frozen, Serena with wide-eyed shock on her face, her arms still raised, blood pouring from her mouth and gushing from her chest where the long dagger had run it clean through, then Kane yanked his arm back and Serena crumbled to the ground, her power gone, nothing more than an empty shell. The Coven of the Ravens was no more.

Maddy collapsed to her knees, sobbing.

~*~

Kane led her up the driveway, his strong arm around her waist. She could barely stand on her own, feeling weak and helpless. He'd explained to her that it was partly exerting so much energy for such a long time and partly the shock of what she'd witnessed.

"Why did you have to kill her?" Maddy asked, for what felt to her like the hundredth time.

"It had to be done. It wasn't just a case of her life or yours, you must see that. If she'd lived, she would have run and started over somewhere else, building a new coven, maybe even taking your sister with her. We barely scratched the surface of the things she and her coven did over the years, and if I sat down and told you all of them, you would have a better understanding of why it was so necessary, why I was even here in the first place. There are millions of evil witches in the world, Maddy. The time of a witch hunter is precious, and we must prioritize. The Coven of the Ravens was a priority, especially once they'd lured the last remaining Stonehers into their midst."

"But I might have found a way to win, to defeat her and still bind her."

"Not in that time and place," Kane shook his head in sadness. "If your parents hadn't made the decision they did and you'd lived the life you were meant to live, then I would agree that you could have done it. Even if we'd had more time to develop and practice your skills, you might have been capable of an instant binding, but you'd poured so much into the spell already and I could feel that you were weakening and wouldn't be able to keep it up much longer, let alone immediately respond to protect yourself against her."

"I failed," she said, utterly miserable.

"You didn't fail," he replied sternly. "You saved the life of your sister, you bound around forty people, including the majority of a powerful coven, saving their lives as well, I might add, and you protected yourself against attack. These things take time, Maddy, a whole lifetime, and yet, you achieved all that after only one month. You did amazingly well, and you should be proud of yourself." He lowered his voice, his tone turning tender. "I know your parents would have been."

Maddy nodded and wiped tears of sorrow and exhaustion from her face. She accepted his words, knowing they were the highest praise he could possibly give. "So, what happens now?"

"For you, not a lot. I'll deal with Serena and remove all traces of evidence. She'll disappear like so many others from this town before her, except by my hand instead of hers. It's what I'm trained for, after all. No one who was there last night will ever be able to access any of their abilities while the binding spell holds. I would suggest you redo the spell every six months or so, just to make sure it stays strong and holds true. No matter where they are, now that it's in place, the magic to renew it will always find them. Serena was the last Rockwell, and now that she's gone, the line is gone for good. It's over."

While they'd been talking, they'd made it inside the house and had now reached the kitchen. Kane flipped on the light. They were both startled to see Allie and Cheryl huddled together there in the dark, still wearing only their ceremonial robes. They turned frightened faces towards them as they entered.

"I didn't know Serena was evil," Allie said with a sob. "I didn't know before now, Maddy, I swear it! I believed Serena when she said she could make me a witch and I could help people. I didn't know, I promise I didn't know!"

As exhausted as she was, Maddy released herself from Kane's support, holding out her arms to her sister. Allie flung herself into them, hugging her tightly, sobs wracking her body. "Hush, it's okay; I know you didn't. There was no way you could have known. I don't blame you; no one blames you."

"What about me?" Cheryl asked in a small voice, her eyes focused on Kane. "You're a witch hunter, aren't you? Are you going to kill us all?"

Kane shook his head. "While your powers remain bound, there's no need for any more bloodshed here. You're safe from me unless that ever changes."

"I'll make sure that never happens," Maddy assured him.

"Good. Cheryl, come with me. I'll take you home. I think the Stonehers have a lot to talk about."

Cheryl rose and moved towards him, cautiously keeping her distance just in case. Kane placed a hand on her upper arm and guided her to the door. "I'd best go," he said to Maddy. "I have duties to attend to."

She nodded, and he turned away. "Wait!" she called, and he turned with a questioning expression. "One more thing. The binding, did that include Allie?"

"Yes, it did. You might want to look into removing that one day. I'm certain there will be something in the Book of Shadows to guide you."

Maddy gave him a tired smile. "Maybe one day, but then again, maybe not. It depends if she's good or not. Will I see you again?"

"Of course," Kane said. "I'm taking you both out for dinner tomorrow night. Now, how about some tea?"

"That is the best idea I've heard in a while," Maddy said.

Allie rose and set the kettle to boil. After taking out three mugs, she reached into the cupboard, bringing down a box. She turned to Maddy. "Herbal from Salt 'n' Sage?"

"Not on your life!"

~*~

Allie retreated back to her room, feeling like a third wheel with her sister making googly eyes at Kane. She still felt a bit uneasy about the man; something about him made her feel uneasy.

Serena told her that he would be coming for her. For all of them if they didn't listen to her.

She turned out to be the bad guy. But still, the power she had.

Allie reached under her bed and pulled out the spell book that Serena had given to her as a gift. The cover had been etched in ancient symbols; she felt a tingle rush up her fingers and arms the moment she touched it.

"You can feel it, can't you?" She remembered Serena asking her that question.

Allie could only nod in agreement. If her sister had displayed such powers of witchcraft, how much power did Allie possess? They both came from the same bloodline.

"You're so much more powerful than your sister." Serena's words resonated through her head.

She ran her fingers across the binding of the book. Inside, she had the power to change lives at her whim. To do wrong to those who did her wrong. The power to change lives and destinies.

Allie no longer wanted to go to school. To hang out with friends or pursue anything worldly. She only wanted one thing.

To be a witch.

"We don't choose the path," Serena's voice echoed in her head. "The path chooses us."

Allie smiled at the thought.

And opened her spell book.